Eat your Greens

by Geoff Patton
illustrated by David Clarke

RISING ★ STARS

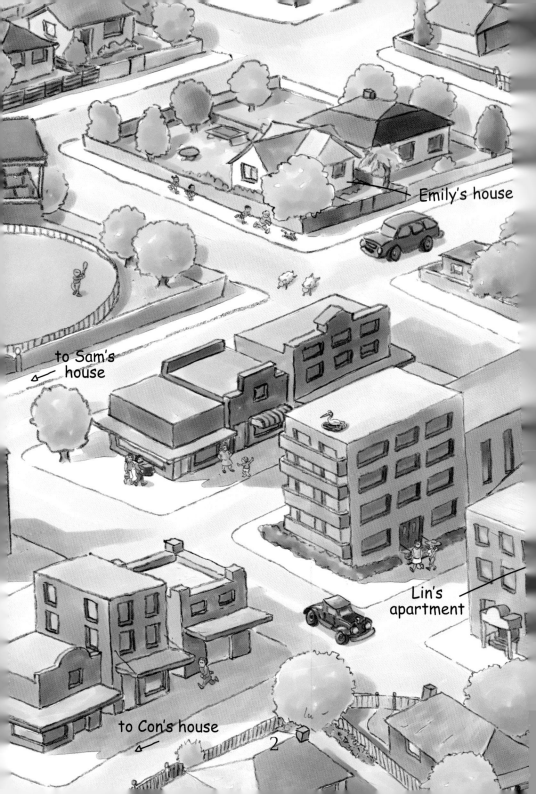

Emily's house

to Sam's house

to Con's house

Lin's apartment

2

Hi. My name is Emily
and this is what my
dinner looks like!

me (Emily)

Molly,
my little sister

4

There are some things I just
don't like. I mean things I *really*
don't like. I have made a list.

Things I Don't Like

cleaning my room—cleaning the dishes—
cleaning of any kind.(yuk)

Doing my homework on Sundays,
or Saturdays. (yuk,yuk)

Cleaning up dog poop.(yuk,yuk,yuk)

Kissing my Great Aunty Jess —She has
very wet lips.(Yuk.yuk.yuk.yuk...)

Eating my greens—vegetables,that is.
(yuk 100 million trillion times)

Chapter 1
Dinner Monday Night – Peas Again!

Every Monday night we have peas.
I don't like peas! I hide my peas
under my potatoes.

Dad says, 'Eat your peas, Emily.'
I say, 'Peas are too round.'
I say, 'I don't like food that is round.'

Dad mashes my peas into
my potatoes.
He says, 'Now they are not round!'

I say, 'I don't like round food,
even when it's mashed.'
'Eat your peas,' says Dad.

I say, 'I would rather clean my room!'
'You can do that *after* dinner,' says Dad.
My dad thinks he is *so* funny.

I close my eyes. I hold my
nose. Gulp. Aaagh!
I wish it was Friday night.

Chapter 2
Dinner Tuesday Night – It's Beans!

On Tuesday night we have beans.
I really don't like beans! I leave
them till last.

Dad says, 'Eat your beans, Emily.'
I say, 'I am allergic to beans.'

Dad says, 'You ate beans when
you were a little girl.'
I say, 'I know. They made my
hair go curly.'

Dad says my hair was always curly
... but I'm not so sure.
'Eat your beans,' says Dad.

I say, 'I would rather do
my homework!'
'You can do that *after* dinner,'
says Dad.
My dad thinks he
is *so* funny.

I close my eyes. I hold my nose.
Gulp. Aaagh!
I wish it was Friday night.

Chapter 3
Dinner Wednesday Night –
It's Cabbage!

On Wednesday night we have cabbage. I really, really don't like cabbage! I leave it till last.

Dad says, 'Eat your cabbage, Emily.' I say, 'Rabbits eat cabbage.'

Dad says, 'Toola Oola eats
her cabbage.'
I say, 'Oh, so that's why
she has such big teeth.'

'Eat your cabbage,' says Dad.

I say, 'I would rather clean up dog poop.'
'You can do that *after* dinner,' says Dad.
My dad thinks he is *so* funny.

I close my eyes. I hold my nose.
Gulp. Aaagh!
I wish it was Friday night.

Chapter 4
Dinner Thursday Night – Lettuce. Aaagh!

On Thursday night we have lettuce. I really, really, really don't like lettuce.

I say, 'Lettuce is salad. I don't like salad.'

Dad says, 'There are lots of children in the world who love to eat lettuce.'
I say, 'Good. They can have mine.'

'Eat your lettuce,' says Dad.

I say, 'I would rather kiss
Great Aunty Jess.'
'You can do that *after* dinner,'
says Dad.
My dad thinks he is *so* funny.

I close my eyes. I hold my nose.
Gulp. Aaagh!
I wish it was Friday night.

Chapter 5
Friday Night!

It's Friday night at last! On Friday night it's *my* turn to make dinner. I always make special burgers.

Dad says he really doesn't like special burgers. He leaves his till last. I say, 'Eat your burger, Dad.'

Dad says, 'Burgers are for kids.'
I say, 'They will make you grow up
big and strong.'

He says he is already grown up ...
but I'm not so sure.

He says he would rather cut
the grass.
'You can do that *after* dinner,' I say.
I am *so* funny.

He closes his eyes.
He holds his nose.
Gulp. Aaagh!
He wishes it was Monday night.

Survival Tips

Tips for surviving green vegetables

1 Peas will roll under potatoes. Hide them and don't eat all your potato.

2 Close your eyes and pretend that you are eating ice-cream.

3 Tell your sister that you will do her homework next week if she eats your beans. It's a good idea to do this the day before school holidays start. Ha, ha, ha.

4 Search the newspaper for a report that says green vegetables are bad for you.

5 Remember you have homework to do after you have eaten everything but your lettuce.

6 Get your dad to make lettuce ice-cream. It may not be nice but it can't be as bad as the real thing.

Riddles and Jokes

Emily   Dad, Dad, there is a fly
in my peas!

Dad   Don't worry, Emily, the spider
on your chops will get it.

Emily   Dad, Dad, these peas
taste funny.

Dad   Why aren't you laughing then?

Emily   Why is a pea small and green?

Dad   I don't know. Why?

Emily   Because if it was big and red
it would be a fire engine.

Emily   Dad, Dad, there is a bug in
my beans.

Dad   Quiet. Your sister will want
one too.